THE
IMPOSSIBLE
RIDDLE

THE IMPOSSIBLE

WRITTEN BY *Ellen Jackson*

ILLUSTRATED BY *Alison Winfield*

RIDDLE

WHISPERING COYOTE PRESS, INC.

Boston

Published by Whispering Coyote Press, Inc.
480 Newbury Street, Danvers, MA 01923
Text copyright © 1995 by Ellen Jackson
Illustrations by Alison Winfield for Arkadia Illustration and Design Ltd. copyright © 1995
by Whispering Coyote Press

Printed in Hong Kong by South China Printing Company(1988)Ltd.
Book production and design by Our House
10 9 8 7 6 5 4 3 2 1

Library of Congress Cataloging-in-Publication Data
Jackson, Ellen B., 1943-
The impossible riddle / written by Ellen Jackson; illustrated by Alison Winfield.
p. cm.
Summary: The tsar of Russia loves his daughter and her potato pancakes so much that he
will not allow her to marry, but finally a handsome young suitor outsmarts him.
ISBN 1-879085-93-3; $14.95
[1. Riddles—Fiction. 2. Kings, queens, rulers, etc.—Fiction. 3. Russia—Fiction.]
I. Winfield, Alison, ill. II. Title.
PZ7.J13247Im 1995
[E]—dc20   94-48810
                                          CIP
                                          AC

To Sally Hertz. Thanks.
—E.J.

Dedicated with thanks to my family and friends
—A.W.

Mighty

Mighty Nicholas, the tsar of all the Russias, loved three things above all else—his daughter, potato pancakes, and riddles.

One day when Nicholas was riding near the town of Walovka, he saw a farmer sweating and fretting as he plowed a field.

"My good man," called the tsar from his carriage window. "Please explain this mystery. How can it be that the hair on your head is gray, but the hair in your beard is black?"

The old

farmer scratched his ear. In truth he didn't know the answer to the tsar's question, but he *did* know that the great tsar must be answered.

"My beard didn't start growing until I was a young man, your excellency. Therefore the hair on my head is older than the hair in my beard, and it is for that reason that it is now gray."

"What a clever answer!" said the tsar. "I come this way once a year. Promise me that you will not discuss this matter with anyone else until you have seen my face one hundred times. For your trouble, here is a ruble."

The farmer promised that he would keep silent, and the tsar drove away chuckling to himself.

hen he

arrived at his palace in St. Petersburg, Tsar Nicholas ordered his daughter, Katarina, to cook up a plate of potato pancakes. He was hungry after his journey.

"Ah, Katarina, no one makes these as well as you," said the tsar.

"I would be happy to teach your cooks to make potato pancakes, Father," said Katarina. "Then you could turn your attention to finding me a royal husband."

"Oh, no, no, Katarina," said the tsar. "There is no king, prince, or duke good enough for you. It's better that you stay here with me. I don't want your potato pancakes wasted on some lout who might not appreciate them."

But Katarina begged and pleaded until the tsar agreed at last to find a husband for her.

ne by
one, royal suitors began to arrive in St. Petersburg. First came the king of France, a small man with piggy eyes, who was dressed in knee breeches and a swallow-tailed coat.

Shortly after his arrival, the king was ushered into the Great Hall.

"I am here to ask permission to marry your daughter and make her my queen," said the king, kneeling before the tsar.

"Indeed!" said the tsar. "Not just anyone will do for my Katarina. The man she marries must know a thing or two about riddles. Answer this: There is an old farmer who lives a day's ride from here. The hair on his head is gray, yet his beard is still black. How do you explain this mystery?"

"How? How indeed...?" stammered the king, wringing his hands. But try as he might, he could not answer the riddle, and so he returned to France.

Next came the crown prince of Norway. He was hairy, and lumpy, and he had a laugh like a horse. The crown prince had brought a fan of white eagle feathers to present to the tsar's daughter.

"Answer this and prove your worthiness," commanded the tsar after he had greeted the prince. "There is an old farmer who lives a day's ride from here. The hair on his head is gray, yet his beard is still black. How do you explain this mystery?"

"The explanation will come to me in a minute," said the crown prince, picking at his beard. But he could not answer the tsar's riddle either, and the next day he returned to Norway without the lovely Katarina.

At this

rate, I'll never be married," muttered Katarina to herself. That evening she put hot peppers into her potato pancakes.

"Ah, potato pancakes with hot peppers! How tasty! No one but you would have thought of that, Katarina," said the tsar.

Late the next afternoon, Prince Egon of Denmark arrived in St. Petersburg. Like the others, he had come to ask for Katarina's hand in marriage.

The handsome young prince had wavy black hair and a pleasant manner, and Katarina was very taken with him. That evening she sent her maidservant to summon Egon to her reception room.

I **would** gladly accept you as my husband," Katarina told the prince. "But, alas, my father will never allow it. Tomorrow he will ask you a stupid but impossible riddle about an old farmer he saw somewhere near Walovka. Even I don't know the answer." Then she told Egon the riddle.

gazed at Katarina. He had already learned to love her potato pancakes, which had been served at dinner, and now he was falling in love with her. Moreover, he was not the sort of prince to be stopped by an impossible riddle.

Egon

Early the next morning he rode his horse to Walovka and found the farmer with the black beard and gray hair. The old man was busy plowing his field, just as he had been doing on the day the tsar first spoke to him.

I will give you one hundred gold coins if you will answer a question for me," said Prince Egon. "Why is the hair in your beard still black while the hair on your head has gone gray?"

The old farmer began to tremble. Here was trouble knocking at his door. But how those gold coins gleamed! As he counted out the hundred coins, the old man thought of all the fine things that money could buy.

"I'm only a poor, ignorant peasant," said the farmer to Prince Egon. "But yes, I will answer your question."

Prince Egon

hurriedly returned to St. Petersburg and went before the tsar to ask for Katarina's hand in marriage.

"I love my daughter very much, not to mention that she makes the best potato pancakes in all of Russia," said the tsar. "So I must test you to see if you are worthy of such a prize. Answer this: Near the village of Walovka lives an old farmer. The hair on his head is gray, yet his beard is still black. Explain this mystery!"

Without hesitating Prince Egon answered, "The farmer's beard didn't start growing until he was already a young man. By that time the hair on his head was already many years old. Therefore the gray hair on his head is older than the black hair in his beard. It makes perfect sense."

"**W**hat?" shrieked the tsar. "That farmer must have given you the answer. I'll have him hanged! Order my carriage at once!"

A few minutes later the tsar and two soldiers were on their way to Walovka.

The tsar found the poor old man working in his field, as usual.

"I've lost my dear daughter, thanks to you!" thundered the tsar. "Didn't I tell you to keep this matter a secret?"

"You did, Excellency," said the man. "But you also said it was a secret only until I had seen you one hundred times."

"You know very well that you only saw me once!" said the tsar, turning to his men. "String him up immediately!"

"But I *have* seen you one hundred times," said the old man. "I will show you."

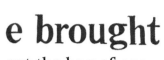**e brought** out the bag of one hundred gold coins. On each gold coin was an image of the tsar.

"I looked at every one of these coins as I counted them. On each is your likeness. I have, indeed, seen you one hundred times," said the old man. "Was I wrong to take you at your word?"

"No! No!" admitted the tsar. "But what am I to do? I have lost my dear Katarina."

The old man looked up at the tsar with a twinkle in his eye.

"Now here is a riddle for *you*. How is it that a tree can be wiser than the tsar?" asked the farmer, pointing to a large tree that was growing by the side of the road.

"I don't know," said the tsar. He was not feeling the least bit wise.

"Look closely," said the farmer. "This tree has many leaves. The leaves are like the tree's children. All summer long they provide nourishment to their father, the tree.

"Yet in autumn the tree lets them go. One by one, they fall to the ground. Over time they enrich the soil so that new life can grow and the earth will be green and beautiful in years to come..."

The tsar and the farmer watched a leaf flutter to the ground.

"It is time to let go," said the tsar quietly.

**nd so**
it was that three
weeks later Katarina
and Prince Egon were
married with the tsar's
blessing. The tsar
never ate potato pancakes again,
except on occasions when Katarina
and Prince Egon visited him. At
those times the tsar was so busy
playing with his grandchildren that
he hardly noticed what was served
for dinner.

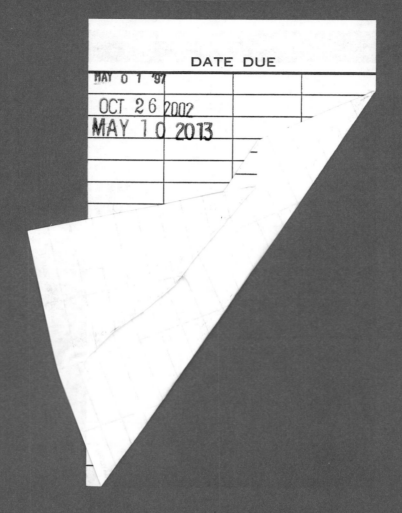

DATE DUE

MAY 0 1 '97		
OCT 26 2002		
MAY 1 0 2013		